Seraph Creative is a collective of artists, writers, theologians & illustrators who desire to see the body of Christ grow into full maturity, walking in their inheritance as Sons of God on the Earth.

Sign up to our newsletter to know about future exciting releases.

Visit our website : www.seraphcreative.org

The Lion & The Lamb

Written by Joey LeTourneau

Illustrations created by Galilee LeTourneau using MidJourney AI

Aliyah was a very special girl with a very special stuffed
friend. And together, they have a very special story.

Lovie wasn't just a stuffed lamb
but a great comfort to Aliyah
and went with her everywhere
she went. Lovie accompanied
Aliyah to the grocery store,
did school with her, and even
brushed her teeth with her!

Aliyah took Lovie everywhere,
and everywhere they went,
Aliyah always found Lovie's
protective presence and his
comforting cuddles.

Aliyah was also a very faithful little girl. There were two things Aliyah did every night before bed. She would find her Lovie — no matter where she had placed him in their adventures that day. And just prior to lying down to sleep, she would look up to God to pray.

With these two bedtime routines every night, Aliyah had the best sleeps and the most wonderful dreams of the adventures that she and Lovie couldn't fit into their day.

Sometimes Aliyah and Lovie would have a
tea party with the Prime Minister.

Other nights she and Lovie would be off
to safari the vast savannah of Africa.

And one night Aliyah and Lovie drove the fire truck
and were the heroes that saved an entire family from a
horrible house fire.

Most of the time, Aliyah and Lovie spent their nights on hot,
sandy beaches or...

...picking luscious fruit in a woodsy berry patch.

But their favorite thing to do together, whether day or night, was to paint their beautiful art together. Lovie was a tough critic in her dreams, but Aliyah was a wonderful and creative artist — both awake and in her sleep.

However, one night did not go as the rest. Aliyah was so tired that after she grabbed her Lovie from the day's adventures, she stumbled past her nighttime prayers and splattered into bed straight into a deep sleep.

That night, Aliyah had a terrible dream. She was walking
through one of the berry patches she and Lovie visited
often, but Lovie was nowhere to be found.
She was alone, and afraid.

It was getting dark, and Aliyah's fear started to grow when she heard footsteps behind her. She saw a giant, beastly shadow leaning out from behind the forest. She ran towards a big rock to hide behind, took a deep breath and wished Lovie was there to protect and comfort her. She could feel a towering presence on the other side of the big rock.

She peered to her left. Then leaned to her right. And that's when she looked up and saw a massive lion on top of the rock, watching every move she made.

Aliyah woke up with a fright, rescued from her dream yet still feeling like it was very real. Lovie was there on her bed; but had not been in her dream when she needed him most. "Please, Lovie," she said, "never leave me like that again!"

After another full day of school, chores and daytime adventures with Lovie, Aliyah was ready for bed. Well, it was time for bed, but she wasn't so sure that she was ready to go to sleep, afraid to face yet another terrible dream.

But as usual, except for the night before, she got down on her knees, said her prayers and then Aliyah pleaded with Lovie not to forsake her that night wherever they went. She tucked Lovie under her arm and fell fast asleep, not knowing what might come next.

To her relief, Aliyah's dreams found her and Lovie skipping rope in the park. They were having so much fun, laughing and playing. But then, suddenly, Lovie was gone! "How could you leave me like that," Aliyah cried aloud. "Lovie, where are you?! Please come back, quickly!"

Aliyah looked up from her cry and her heart became flush with fear. Lovie had not answered, but the Lion was back, and this time was running full speed in her direction...

...She ran up to the jungle gym as fast as she could,
hid inside the tunnel and prayed to wake up quickly.

And wake up she did, breathing heavily, frantically feeling around the bed
looking for Lovie. And there he was, he had fallen off the bed and was lying
peacefully on the floor. Maybe she had dropped him in the night and that's
why Lovie hadn't come when she called? Aliyah wasn't sure, but she knew she
didn't like the fear she kept feeling.

Aliyah shook off the fright and managed to have a good day. As the night drew near, she tried to prepare herself and gird up the strength of her spirit. "I'm okay," she'd repeat. "You're always with me." She would declare.

Aliyah made her way to bed, never letting Lovie out of her sight. She took a deep breath, got down on her knees and prayed fervently not to be left alone. She looked at Lovie and said sternly, "You got that? I need you with me!" Aliyah nodded Lovie's head with a firm yes towards herself and let out a deep sigh as she climbed under her covers with Lovie grasped tightly under her arm.

Aliyah was whisked quickly into her dreams. Laughing and playing, she and Lovie were skipping through a meadow. That's when Lovie suggested they play hide and seek. It was Lovie's turn to hide, and Aliyah's turn to seek, so Aliyah counted loudly while Lovie tip-toed towards the forest.

Aliyah knew that Lovie liked the berries in the forest so she was sure where she would find him. She heard some rustling on the other side of a bush and jumped around to surprise Lovie. But it was Aliyah who was surprised, and it was not a good surprise either. Lovie was gone, maybe even eaten, Aliyah worried by this growling pack of wolves — their sites now set on Aliyah!

Aliyah tried to run but didn't know how she would get away. She ran past the big rock nearby and that's when she saw him, that fearful lion she had run from the two times before. "Wolves and a lion?" Aliyah gasped and kept running with the wolves closing in from behind.

The lion pounced, but not on Aliyah. It jumped right on
top of that vicious pack of wolves, and there was quite the
battle. The lion was much larger, but the wolves were many.
She couldn't believe the lion would fight for her like this,
and one by one the wolves ran off, far from Aliyah.

But that's where she found the lion, barely alive and scarcely
breathing. In the moments she had needed him most Lovie
had seemingly disappeared, but the lion she had been so
afraid of the two nights before was there right on time
to save her. She missed Lovie, but she offered the lion a
thankful hug as it lay there in the field.

Aliyah woke up somber, but thankful. She looked down for
Lovie, but Lovie was still nowhere to be found. However,
in her left arm was tucked a big, snuggly, soft lion. The
tag around his neck read: Lovie the Lion.

That's when Aliyah realized that during those first two bad dreams, when she thought Lovie hadn't come, he had been with her the whole time, only in a way that she had not yet recognized. But now Aliyah knew that Lovie was much more than she ever knew or imagined; he was both a Lion and a Lamb.

Lovie was never the same,
and neither was Aliyah.

Joey and his wife, Destiny, have been married for 23 years. They have eight children and two grandchildren. As a family, they have both lived, and traveled, all around the world, empowering people to discover and live out who they were created to be. Joey has authored eleven books, and three children's books. As a family, they write and create to give life to a generation who will shine in the world.

To see other books and projects by the author, please visit: LeTourneau Creative

LeTourneaucreative.com

www.ingramcontent.com/pod-product-compliance
Lightning Source LLC
Chambersburg PA
CBHW042122030726
47599CB00002B/310